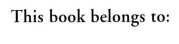

A catalogue record for this book is available
from the British Library

Published by Ladybird Books Ltd
A subsidiary of the Penguin Group
A Pearson Company
© LADYBIRD BOOKS LTD MCMXCVIII

LADYBIRD and the device of a Ladybird are trademarks of
Ladybird Books Ltd Loughborough Leicestershire UK

Saving Suki

written by Elizabeth Dale
illustrated by David Kearney

Jenny was having a perfect Sunday. Her dad was a vet and her mum was a veterinary nurse and Sunday was the one day her parents managed to take time off from work. And now, after a huge meal, she and her family were going for a walk along the beach.

Jenny's little sister Caroline, who was always full of energy, ran on ahead. Suddenly she stopped and pointed to a dark shape by the water's edge.

"Look!" she cried. "Come and see!"

As Jenny and her family approached,
they realised that the small, dark
shape was a bird. It struggled to
the water, and tried to fly off. But its
wings flapped uselessly.

"It's covered in oil!" cried Matthew,
Jenny's brother.

Jenny gazed in horror. It was true.
The little bird was shiny and black.
Only its eyes could be seen glinting
amongst a mass of oily feathers.

"The poor thing!" said Jenny.
"What is it?"

"It's a herring gull," said her dad,
picking the bird up gently.
"Let's get him home
and clean him up."

Back at the surgery, the children watched as their dad wiped the oil away from the gull's eyes and beak. Then he put a tube into its mouth.

"That looks painful," said Matthew.

"If he's swallowed any oil, this fluid will flush it out," said Mr Walsh. "It could save his life."

Finally the poor bird was put in
a warm cage to recover.

"I wonder if there are any more
birds covered in oil?" Jenny asked.

"I didn't see any," said her dad.
"I think this was probably just
a small spill from a boat."

"But there might be other birds!"
argued Jenny. "We just might not
have seen them!"

"It's possible," said her dad.

"Can we go and look?"
asked Matthew.

"Teatime!" called Mrs Walsh.

"Oh, Mum!" cried Jenny. "How can we eat, when birds might be drowning because of the oil!"

"Have some tea," said her mum, "and then we'll all go and look."

The whole family searched the beach without success.

"I don't think there are any more birds," said Jenny's dad, looking through his binoculars.

"Not that we've seen!" murmured Jenny.

How could they really be sure?

Before Jenny went to bed, she went to see the gull. Her dad had just cleaned his feathers and he looked a lot better. He even looked like a gull!

"Will he be all right?" she asked her dad.

"I think he'll be fine," he said. "We'll just watch over him for a few days."

That night, Jenny had a very
vivid dream.

"Where are you?" she cried in
her sleep. "I can't see you!"

Her mum rushed in.

"What's the matter, Jenny?"
she asked.

"I had a dream!" Jenny whispered. "Oh, Mum! Something in the sea was calling to me, but I couldn't reach it. It needs my help!"

"There, there!" said her mum, soothingly. "It's nothing. You were just thinking about the gull we found today."

But was she? Jenny lay in her bed, unable to sleep. The cry in her dream had been so real, so desperate. What if it meant something? What if some other poor creature needed rescuing?
She had to do something!

Straight after school, Jenny, her brother and sister and her friend Tom went back to the beach with Mr Walsh. But they saw no more injured animals.

"I have to get back for evening surgery," said Mr Walsh.
"We'll have to go now."

"Five more minutes, please?" begged Jenny.

"All right," smiled her dad.

Suddenly Tom cried out,
"Look! Over there!"

And as they looked to where Tom
was pointing, they all saw a dark
shape moving by the water's edge.

"It's a young seal," said Jenny's dad, "and it's covered in oil!"

"Oh, no!" cried Jenny. "We must save it!"

"I'll have to fetch my rescue equipment," said Mr Walsh. "Keep an eye on it whilst I'm gone, but don't go too close. Seals have a nasty bite!"

Soon Mr Walsh returned. He
approached the seal slowly
and reached out towards it with
a grasper. Once the loop of rope
was safely over the animal's head,
he put the seal into a cage and the
children helped to carry it back to
the car.

At the surgery, Jenny watched her mum and dad wash off the oil.

"It seems very weak," she said.

"She is," said Mr Walsh, "but at least she doesn't seem to have swallowed much oil and she's young and strong. I think we rescued her just in time."

Jenny smiled – thanks to her dream!

Jenny called the seal Suki. She
had lovely soft fur and beautiful,
big dark eyes that gazed sadly up
at her. Whenever Jenny came into
the room, Suki called to her with
a strange kind of bark.

Gradually, Suki grew stronger. Jenny loved to talk to her, and Suki seemed to listen, as though she understood. Finally, Suki was strong enough to move into the big pool outside the surgery. Matthew and Jenny threw fish to her. Suki caught them before they even reached the water.

She flicked her flipper excitedly, splashing the children with water.

"Thanks, Suki!" cried Matthew, jumping back.

And Suki made her funny barking noise, as if to say 'It's a pleasure!'.

"Suki is ready to go back to the wild," announced Mr Walsh one morning.

"Oh, no!" Jenny cried.

"Jenny, it's not fair to keep her here," explained her dad. "She's a wild animal. She needs to go back to the sea."

Jenny frowned, but she knew her dad was right.

The whole family and Tom came
to watch Mr Walsh set Suki free
on the beach. Once out of her cage,
Suki just lay on the sand, her nose
twitching as she smelt the sea. And
then she looked back at Jenny.

"Go on, Suki! Back to the sea!" urged Jenny.

Suki turned and moved clumsily down the beach.

She reached the water's edge and in an instant became a beautiful, graceful animal. Suddenly she dived under the water and was gone. Everyone cheered and turned to go. But Jenny kept on watching.

Then, in the distance, Suki's head popped up again and she looked back.

"Goodbye, Suki!" said Jenny, quietly. "I'm going to miss you."

Jenny thought about Suki all the time, willing her to be safe.

"Do you think she's all right?" Jenny asked her dad, anxiously.

"I expect so," said her dad. "But it's always hard for a young animal adjusting back to the wild."

Every night after school, Tom and Jenny went down to the beach, looking for Suki. But there was no sign of her.

"Cheer up, Jenny!" said Tom. "Just because you can't see Suki, it doesn't mean there's anything wrong. She might have swum miles away!"

But Jenny shook her head. Suki wouldn't have gone far away. This was her home.

She was just turning to go, when she heard a sudden splash.

"Don't throw stones, Tom!" she said crossly.

"I didn't!" cried Tom. "Look!"

Jenny looked towards the water, and there she saw Suki darting through the waves.

"Oh, Suki! You're okay!" cried Jenny. Suki's head popped up and she looked at Jenny with her big, dark eyes. Then she barked her funny little bark, as if to say 'Of course I'm okay!'.

And Jenny and Tom laughed, for it was obviously true.

Mr Walsh tells you more about... helping oiled animals

Oil spillages, however large or small, are very dangerous to birds and animals. Just one drop of oil on their fur or feathers lets water to their skin and they can get very cold indeed.

When all the oil has been washed away, the bird needs to dry out under a warm lamp. Next, it is allowed to swim in clean water. At first it keeps getting wet and coming out to dry. After a few days the feathers are back to normal and the bird can usually swim for several hours without getting wet. Then at last, it can be released back into the wild.

Meet the characters…

Mr Walsh
a vet

Mrs Walsh
a veterinary nurse

Jenny Walsh
nine years old

Matthew Walsh
eleven years old

Caroline Walsh
four years old

Tom Henderson
nine years old and Jenny's best friend

Jepp
the family collie dog

If a bird swallows oil, it has to be fed through a special tube which goes down its throat and into its stomach. Once the bird has recovered, the feathers can be cleaned with washing up liquid.